GEO

4-16
Lexile: _____

AR/BL: ___3.1___

AR Points: ___0.5___

Cooperation

A Level Three Reader

By Kathryn Kyle

On the cover...
These children are cooperating to color a map.

Published by The Child's World®, Inc.
PO Box 326
Chanhassen, MN 55317-0326
800-599-READ
www.childsworld.com

Special thanks to the Matsuyama, Melaniphy, and Sanks families and the staff and students of Alessandro Volta Elementary School for their help and cooperation in preparing this book.

Photo Credits
© Bettmann/CORBIS: 22, 25
© 2003 Charles Thatcher/Stone: cover
© David Young-Wolff/PhotoEdit: 6
© Deborah Davis/PhotoEdit: 3
© Michael Newman/PhotoEdit: 13
© Michelle Bridwell/PhotoEdit: 10
© Romie Flanagan: 5, 9, 17, 18, 21, 26
© Tom McCarthy/PhotoEdit: 14

Project Coordination: Editorial Directions, Inc.
Photo Research: Alice K. Flanagan

Library of Congress Cataloging-in-Publication Data
Kyle, Kathryn.
Cooperation / by Kathryn Kyle.
    p. cm. — (Wonder books)
Includes index.
Summary: Easy-to-read scenarios, such as cleaning up after supper or
playing on a team, provide lessons in cooperation.
ISBN 1-56766-086-X (alk. paper)
1. Cooperativeness—Juvenile literature. [1. Cooperativeness.]
I. Title. II. Wonder books (Chanhassen, Minn.)
BJ1533.C74 .K95 2002
179'.9—dc21
                        2001007948

What is **cooperation**? Cooperation is working together to get something done. Cooperation helps us all in our everyday life.

At home, we rake leaves in the fall. It is a big job. The job is easier when more people help. Cooperation is working with your family to rake the leaves.

After supper, everyone wants to go have fun. But first it is time to clean up. Cleaning up is quick if everyone cooperates. One person clears the table. Another cleans up the dishes. Someone else puts the food away.

Cooperation is an important part of playing on a team. On a baseball team, all the players need to work together. The more they cooperate, the better they play. **Teamwork** is another word for cooperation.

At school, your group is putting on a play. This takes cooperation. There are many jobs. Some people will act in the play. They must **memorize** their lines. Others work on the costumes and the set.

Playing music together is another way to cooperate. In a band, some people play **instruments** while others sing. Cooperating will make the song sound pretty. If the band does not cooperate, the song will sound terrible!

Building things with friends takes cooperation. Building a sand castle is lots of fun. You and your friends can work together to build a sand castle.

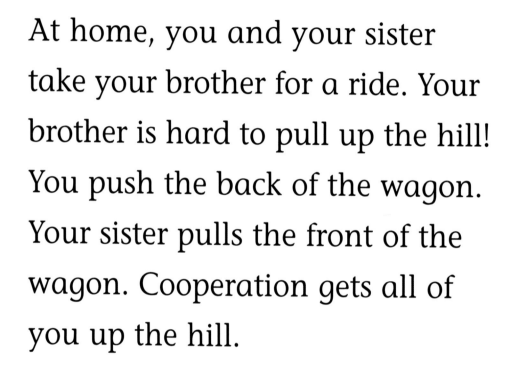

At home, you and your sister take your brother for a ride. Your brother is hard to pull up the hill! You push the back of the wagon. Your sister pulls the front of the wagon. Cooperation gets all of you up the hill.

18

Sometimes cooperation means following the rules. On the bus, it is important to listen to the bus driver. The bus driver has rules that keep us safe on the bus. Cooperating with the driver keeps everyone safe.

Cooperation can also mean sharing. Your group at school is doing a project. To do a good job, everyone must cooperate. One person needs to use your scissors. You share the scissors. Your group finishes the project!

Many people in history have gotten things done through cooperation. One of these people was Thomas Jefferson. In 1776, Jefferson wrote the **Declaration of Independence**. This is an important **document** in American history. It said that the American **colonies** were free from the British government.

This is a picture of Thomas Jefferson.

Jefferson had to include the ideas of many people. This was not always easy to do. Jefferson worked with many other people to complete the Declaration of Independence. By cooperating with others, Thomas Jefferson helped make history.

This drawing shows Thomas Jefferson working with others to write the Declaration of Independence.

Cooperation is important at home, at school, and in your community. Working together helps people get many things done. Cooperation can also be fun. How have you cooperated with other people today?

At Home

- Help your parents make breakfast or dinner.

- Work with your brother or sister to clean up the house.

- Enjoy putting together a jigsaw puzzle with your family.

At School

- Work with your classmates to clean your table in the cafeteria after lunch.

- Work with a friend on a class project.

- Listen to your teacher's instructions and follow them carefully so things run smoothly in class.

In Your Community

- Volunteer to help collect canned goods for a local food pantry.

- Work with your neighbors to shovel the sidewalks after a snowstorm.

- Help your older neighbors do their yard work.

Glossary

colonies (KOL-uh-neez)
Colonies are lands ruled by a faraway country.

cooperation (koh-op-uh-RAY-shun)
Cooperation means working together to get something done.

Declaration of Independence
(dek-luh-RAY-shun of in-deh-PEN-dens)
The Declaration of Independence is a paper that announced the freedom of the thirteen American colonies from British rule. It was signed on July 4, 1776.

document (DOK-yoo-ment)
A document is a piece of paper with important information on it.

instruments (IN-struh-mentz)
Instruments are objects you use to make music.

memorize (MEM-uh-rize)
When you memorize something, you learn it by heart.

teamwork (TEEM-werk)
Teamwork is when a group of people work together to get something done.

Index

To Find Out More

Books

Adler, David A. *A Picture Book of Thomas Jefferson.* New York: Holiday House, 1991.

Marzollo, Jean, and Dan Marzollo. *Hockey Hero.* New York: Cartwheel Books, 1999.

Quakenbush, Robert. *Pass the Quill, I'll Write a Draft: A Story of Thomas Jefferson.* New York: Pippin Press, 1989.

Stadler, John. *One Seal.* New York: Orchard Books, 1999.

Web Sites

Kids Games Play
http://www.gameskidsplay.net/
For the directions and rules to all kinds of playground games.

KidsHealth for Kids
http://kidshealth.org/kid/feeling/home_family/single_parents.html
To learn about cooperation in your own family.

Note to Parents and Educators

Welcome to Wonder Books®! These books provide text at three different levels for beginning readers to practice and strengthen their reading skills. Additionally, the use of nonfiction text provides readers the valuable opportunity to *read to learn*, not just to learn to read.

These leveled readers allow children to choose books at their level of reading confidence and performance. Nonfiction Level One books offer beginning readers simple language, word choice, and sentence structure as well as a word list. Nonfiction Level Two books feature slightly more difficult vocabulary, longer sentences, and longer total text. In the back of each Nonfiction Level Two book are an index and a list of books and Web sites for finding out more information. Nonfiction Level Three books continue to extend word choice and length of text. In the back of each Nonfiction Level Three book are a glossary, an index, and a list of books and Web sites for further research.

State and national standards in reading and language arts emphasize using nonfiction at all levels of reading development. Wonder Books® fill the historical void in nonfiction material for primary grade readers with the additional benefit of a leveled text.

About the Author

Kathryn Kyle has taught elementary school and writes extensively for children. She lives in Minnesota.